DEVELOPING READER
LEVEL **2**
250-750 WORDS

The Scary Safari

By Gail Herman
Illustrated by Duendes del Sur

SCHOLASTIC INC.
New York   Toronto   London   Auckland   Sydney
Mexico City   New Delhi   Hong Kong   Buenos Aires

ISBN 13: 978-0-545-08168-9
ISBN 10: 0-545-08168-8

Designed by Michael Massen

12 11 10 9 8 7 6 5 4 3 2   8 9 10/0

Printed in the U.S.A.
First printing, September 2008

"Here we are!" said Fred. "Super Safari Park!"
"Where you see animals up close," Velma read the sign.
"And from your car!" added Daphne.

Grrr!

"Ro no!" Scooby jumped in fright. "Rion?"

"Not a lion, Scoob, old pal," said Shaggy.

"Just my stomach growling."

The Mystery Machine joined a line of cars.
"This could take a while," Shaggy
whispered to Scooby.
"Like, let's make a snack run!
No one will even know we're gone!"

Quietly, Shaggy and Scooby jumped out.
They piled hot dogs, hamburgers, chips,
and fries onto trays.
Then they sneaked back into the van.

Chomp, chomp, gulp.
Romp, romp, rulp.
The food was all gone.
Now Shaggy and Scooby could see out the window.

"This doesn't look like the ad," said Shaggy.
The park looked like a jungle.
A spooky jungle!

"Zoinks!" cried Shaggy. "Look up, good buddy."
A scary-looking elephant flew over their heads.
"Rhost!" said Scooby.
"Ghost!" agreed Shaggy

Another ghost elephant suddenly appeared.
And another. And another!

They were coming in for a landing —
right next to the van!

Shaggy and Scooby had to get away. Fast!

"Red!" shouted Scooby.
"Fred!" shouted Shaggy.
The driver turned.
It wasn't Fred.
It was a ghost hunter, hunting
ghost elephants . . .

. . . and hunting Shaggy and Scooby!

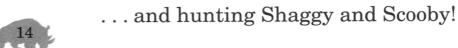

"Like, in here, Scoob!" said Shaggy as he hopped into the cab of empty truck. "We'll lose him quick."

They drove past giraffes and rhinos . . .

. . . and a giant ghost elephant!
This one was even bigger and scarier than the others.

"Raster!" cried Scooby. Shaggy sped faster and faster. Until —

A herd of zebras grazed in front of them. Scooby gulped.

"Come on and run, you guys!" Shaggy pleaded.

"Like, aren't you scared of ghosts?

The first zebra lifted his head.
Then one by one the zebras walked away . . .
only to reveal the ghost hunter!
He was aiming right for them!

"Let's hit the road!" shouted Shaggy.

"*Dooooon't goooooo*," moaned the ghost hunter, following behind.

A moment later, Shaggy grinned.
"We lost him, Scoob!"
Roar!
A lion leaped onto their truck.
They couldn't go anywhere now! And the hunter was coming closer and closer!

"Like, get a move on," shouted Shaggy. "Quit lyin' around!"

ROAR! The lion jumped off. And Shaggy took off. But there was nowhere to go.

They were blocked in every direction!
Ghost elephants chased them from above.
The giant ghost elephant was coming from the side.
And the ghost hunter was gaining on them from behind.

"Like, hold on, Scoob!" Shaggy yelled.
He stepped on the gas.
CRASH!
The truck tore through a gate and
screeched to a stop.

Long spooky arms reached in to pull them out.
"Get lost, ghosts!" said Shaggy.
But the ghosts were strong. As strong as —

"We've got to escape the elephant ghosts!" Scooby pointed his left paw up to the sky. "Those aren't ghosts," said Velma. "They're airplanes from the park, made up to look like elephants. They deliver supplies."

Scooby pointed his right paw at the giant elephant ghost.

"That's a tour boat floating down the park river. It's made up like an elephant, too," Velma went on.

"But there's a ghost hunter!" Shaggy said. "We were in his ghost van!"

Daphne laughed.

"That's the park photographer! With a camera!"

Velma nodded.

"You two must have gotten into his van by mistake."

"Are you guys ready to go on the real safari?" asked Fred.

"Uh, maybe later," said Shaggy.